DANCE

Swing Dancing

by Wendy Garofoli

Consultants:

Cynthia R. Millman
Coauthor,
Frankie Manning: Ambassador of Lindy Hop

Lance Benishek
Dance Historian, Teacher, Choreographer
St. Paul, Minnesota

Capstone *press*®

Mankato, Minnesota

Snap Books are published by Capstone Press,
151 Good Counsel Drive, P.O. Box 669, Mankato, Minnesota 56002.
www.capstonepress.com

Library of Congress Cataloging-in-Publication Data
Garofoli, Wendy.
    Swing dancing : by Wendy Garofoli.
    p. cm. — (Snap Books. Dance)
    Summary: "Describes swing dance, including history and basic
steps" — Provided by publisher.
    Includes bibliographical references and index.
    ISBN-13: 978-1-4296-1350-7 (hardcover)
    ISBN-10: 1-4296-1350-5 (hardcover)
    1. Swing (Dance) — Juvenile literature. I. Title.
GV1796.S85G37 2008
793.31 — dc22   2007031124

Editor: Jennifer Besel

Designer: Veronica Bianchini

Photo Researcher: Jo Miller

Photo Credits: All photos by Capstone Press/Karon Dubke, except:
Corbis/Bettmann, 6–7
Courtesy of the author Wendy Garofoli, 32
Getty Images Inc./AFP/Timothy A. Clary, 27
Ralph Gabriner, 9

Acknowledgements:
Capstone Press would like to thank Morgan Gabse for her assistance preparing this book. Capstone Press would also
like to thank the Dancers Studio in St. Paul, Minnesota, for its assistance.

Capstone Press acknowledges Frankie Manning's autobiography, *Frankie Manning: Ambassador of Lindy Hop,*
cowritten by Cynthia R. Millman, as a source of historical information.

Table of Contents

Swingin' History

Jump up. Kick out your feet.
Spin, twist, and leap.

It's not called swing dancing for nothing. With thrilling twists and driving rhythms, swing dancing burns up the dance floor.

If you like to move, groove, and have fun, then swing dancing is for you. Swing is a dance style that's been around for decades. And you can bet people will be swing dancing for many years to come.

The Swing Family Tree

Swing dance didn't develop all by itself. The partner dances of the 1920s paved the way for modern swing styles. The Charleston featured energetic movements of the arms, legs, and body. The Collegiate, a dance similar to the Charleston, was performed with partners. In the Breakaway, partners separated from each other. The dancers had more freedom to move and improvise. Even today, you'll see hints of the dances of the 1920s in swing dancing.

Swingin' Melodies

Swing music is a style that allows musicians to improvise and have fun with the music. But it also has a strong beat that "swings" listeners from one note to another. Take a listen to "It Don't Mean a Thing If It Ain't Got That Swing" by Duke Ellington. "Jump, Jive, an' Wail" by the Brian Setzer Orchestra is another popular tune. These songs will get big band rhythms into your bones.

The Lindy Hop

Swing's golden era was during the 1930s and '40s. Swing dancers filled the famous Savoy Ballroom in Harlem, New York. Dancers, such as Frankie Manning and George "Shorty" Snowden, lit up the floor with amazing moves.

Incorporating Charleston kicks, fast footwork, and partnering, the Lindy hop became an energetic combination of dances. Manning helped make swing dancing even more exciting when he created the first air step. He sent his partner, Frieda Washington, flying through the air in time with the music. Their over-the-back move inspired dancers across the country to create their own air steps.

Fantastic Frankie

Swing dancing just wouldn't be what it is today if it weren't for Frankie Manning. Manning is often called the Ambassador of Lindy hop. He stunned crowds with his fast feet and amazing moves. When swing dancing was revived in the 1980s, Manning was there to teach and dance. Now in his 90s, Manning still twists and turns around the dance floor.

Rise, Fall, and Rise Again

After the 1940s, the popularity of swing music died down. Rock and roll became popular. In some parts of the United States, people danced to rock and roll music instead of swing. Swing dance lived on in some areas of the country, but its popularity faded.

Then in the 1980s, people got interested in swing again. Swing events began popping up in places like California, Sweden, and London. By 1986, people were looking for ways to learn more about swing dancing. The new swing movement brought Frankie Manning out of retirement. He taught dancers about swing dancing in the 1930s and '40s. When the 1990s rolled around, swing dancing was hot. People around the world were swingin' again.

Swing Time

Now that you're a swing history buff, you're ready to jump, jive, and wail!

Today, dancers itching to swing can't go back to the Savoy Ballroom. But there are many places to learn, watch, and perform swing.

Some dance studios offer swing classes, but they are mostly for adults. Many young dancers learn swing at workshops and camps. Lots of cities have pre-21 clubs where kids can take swing lessons. Many places host swing parties for kids. Instructional videos and Web sites are other ways to learn about swing.

What to Wear

Unlike other dance forms, a leotard and tights are not needed for swing. Instead, wear comfortable clothes that are easy to move in. For practice, both guys and girls can dress in shorts or jeans and T-shirts.

You'll want to dress up when you perform. Girls often wear skirts or dresses. They also wear an undergarment under their skirts called dance pants. Guys can wear pants and a button-down shirt. You can dress in vintage clothes too. Many dancers wear clothes that were popular in the 1930s and '40s.

Dance pants keep you covered when you're twisting and flipping around.

14

More important than the dress code is what you put on your feet. For a sticky floor, grab some shoes with leather or suede soles. If the floor is slick, rubber soles will keep you on your toes.

Sneakers are a great option for practice. When it comes to performances, some women wear heels, but it's not required. All shoes should stay secure on your feet and be comfortable to wear.

Get Ready

Swing is an athletic dance, so your heart will soon be racing. You'll need to be in good shape to keep up with the fast pace of swing. Get yourself in shape by jogging, jumping, or playing sports.

Stretching before you dance is also important. Reach down and touch your toes to stretch your hamstrings. Then reach up to the sky to loosen up your arms. Next, stand with your feet apart and knees slightly bent. Roll your hips in a circle going clockwise and then counterclockwise. You'll use your hips a lot in swing, so it's important to loosen them up.

Ready, Set, Swing

Ready to get out there and show your stuff? Well, grab a partner and let's go.

Swing is a partner dance. You might want to invite a friend to learn swing dance with you. Or you could go to a class and find a partner there.

In swing dancing, one partner leads, while the other follows. The leader directs which steps to do next. If the couple is guy/girl, the guy does the leading and the girl follows. The steps in this book will give you a good idea of what the follower's steps should be. If you're the leader, your footwork will be opposite of what the directions state.

1

The rock step is a basic footwork pattern used in all styles of swing. To rock back, step behind with your right foot then forward with your left foot. To rock forward, step forward first with your right and then back with your left.

2

A Few More Basics

Some basic positioning and footwork will help you get the hang of swing. The basic step is a good move to learn before moving on to harder steps. The move can be completed in six or eight counts and often incorporates a rock step. For a six-count basic step, step on your right foot for two counts. Then step on your left foot for two counts. Finally, rock step back for two counts.

The basic swing out is a signature move in the Lindy hop. It's done as an eight-count step. As the follower, move your feet in this pattern: right, left, right-left-right, left, right, left-right-left. You count the steps like this: one, two, three and four, five, six, seven and eight.

To jazz up your Lindy hop lesson, try a kick away. You simply turn away from your partner and kick out to the side.

Looking for a unique step?

You can do the heels move in place of a rock step. Face your partner and hold hands. Rock back on your heels and bend your body forward toward your partner. Your hips should be sticking out behind you and your weight is on your heels. You can hit this position when performing the Lindy hop.

A fun turn that will get you twisting is the underarm turn. You start standing in a closed position with your partner. Facing each other, the follower's left hand goes on the leader's shoulder. The leader's right hand will be on the follower's waist. Hold your other hands together. Then the leader lifts his left arm to start the step. Next, he moves his right hand behind the follower's shoulder and guides her under his left arm. As she turns around, she'll step away from him and return to the closed position. As you do the underarm turn, your feet can be moving in a basic six-count step.

Air steps are some of the coolest and most recognizable swing moves. These moves are more advanced, though. Only practice them after you have the basics mastered. Be sure to have a teacher or a spotter nearby to catch you if you fall. It's a good idea to use floor mats until you've really gotten the hang of it.

When you see the over-the-back move, you'll understand why Frankie Manning became so popular. To do this step, stand back-to-back with your partner and link arms. As your partner bends down, roll over his back and flip forward. You'll land on your feet facing your partner.

Another fun air step is the straddle. The guy holds the girl's waist while she plants her hands on his shoulders. As she jumps up, she straddles her legs around his waist and he dips her down. Then, using arm strength and momentum, the guy lifts the girl into the air. In the air, the girl kicks her legs up. She lands facing him with both feet together on the floor and knees slightly bent.

Chapter Four

Swing On

Got all that fancy footwork down? Show off your stuff!

After you master some moves, you can show off your stuff at a swing competition. There are many events throughout the country. These events include the World Swing Dance Championships and Swing Dance USA. Competitors may enter at the novice level all the way through to masters.

Some events are combined competitions and workshops. In addition to dancing in front of judges, you can also take classes from swing teachers. These events always feature social dance nights. Competitors get together to just dance and have a blast.

Competitions

There are all sorts of ways to compete in swing dance. You can enter in different styles, levels, and categories. Some competitions even have swing teams where more than one couple performs a routine together. Check each competition's Web site for guidelines.

Get Movin'!

Swing dancing has been around for almost 80 years, and it's still going strong. Swing's golden years might have long passed by, but the dance continues to inspire a whole new generation. Try it for yourself and see. Maybe you'll be swingin' up a storm until you're 90 years old!

Glossary

air step (AIR STEP) — a move in which one partner moves the other partner in the air in time with the music

era (IHR-uh) — a period of time in history

momentum (moh-MEN-tuhm) — the force an object has when it's moving

rhythm (RITH-uhm) — a regular beat in music or dance

spotter (SPOT-uhr) — a person who keeps watch to help prevent injury

vintage (VIN-tij) — from the past

Fast Facts

Today, there are about 10 different styles of swing dancing. The styles look different because the moves were changed as the dance spread around the world.

Swing dancing became famous on the dance floor of the Savoy Ballroom in Harlem, New York. This ballroom was huge. Almost 4,000 people could dance on the floor at once. Two bands would take turns playing so the music never stopped.

In 1927, Charles Lindbergh flew the first solo nonstop flight across the Atlantic Ocean. People were so excited about his success that even a dance was named after him — the Lindy hop!

Read More

Govenar, Alan, ed. *Stompin' at the Savoy: The Story of Norma Miller.* Cambridge, Mass.: Candlewick Press, 2006.

Handyside, Christopher. *Jazz.* A History of American Music. Chicago: Heinemann, 2006.

Hill, Laban Carrick. *Harlem Stomp!: A Cultural History of the Harlem Renaissance.* New York: Little, Brown, 2003.

Internet Sites

FactHound offers a safe, fun way to find Internet sites related to this book. All of the sites on FactHound have been researched by our staff.

Here's how:

1. Visit *www.facthound.com*

2. Choose your grade level.

3. Type in this book ID **1429613505** for age-appropriate sites. You may also browse subjects by clicking on letters, or by clicking on pictures and words.

4. Click on the **Fetch It** button.

Facthound will fetch the best sites for you!

About the Author

Wendy Garofoli is a freelance writer for *Dance Magazine*, *Dance Spirit*, *Dance Retailer News*, and *Cheer Biz News*. She has written other dance titles for Capstone Press, including *Dance Teams*, *Breakdancing*, *Jazz*, *Modern*, and *Irish Step*.

INDEX